"Stop fighting, you two. I just thought of a way you can find out what happened to Jenny's doll!"

Jenny and Jimmy turned to stare at her, forgetting their argument for the moment.

"What are you thinking, Luana?" asked Jimmy.

Jenny narrowed her eyes. "Yes, Luana, what *are* you thinking? And why should I trust you? Whatever scheme you have up your sleeve, I'm sure it's for Jimmy's benefit, not mine. You probably believe him and want to prove he's innocent."

"What I believe won't matter," said Luana. "Because my idea is this: we take your case to court!" Her amber eyes sparkled.

"Court!" the twins exclaimed.

"How would we do that?" Jimmy's forehead puckered.

"Yeah," said Jenny. "What court is going to listen to our case?"

Luana beamed. "A kids' court. A court operated *by* kids *for* kids."

Join the KIDS' COURT & solve these other
mysteries

A KIDS' COURT WHODUNIT

WHODUNIT

THE DOLL DILEMMA

BY CARON PESCATORE

Cover design by Best Page Forward
https://www.bestpageforward.net/

ISBN-13: 978-0997587975

Library of Congress Control Number: 2022902162

LCCN Imprint Name: Caron Pescatore, Fort Lauderdale FL

PESKY BOOKS 4KIDZ

An Imprint of Caron Pescatore, Fort Lauderdale, FL

Published 2022
First edition published May 2016
Second edition published February 2022

Printed in the United States of America

KIDS' COURT STAFF

Luana
Defense Lawyer

Lindsey
Court Reporter

Jake
Court Bailiff

Heather
Judge

Mary Beth
Plaintiff's Lawyer

Ashley
Private Investigator

Phoebe
Private Investigator

For God,
without whom I could not have written this book;
for my husband,
who pushed, cajoled, and encouraged me;
and for my children,
who are my constant source of inspiration.

TABLE OF CONTENTS

CHAPTER 1

A Great Idea!

"THAT'S NOT FAIR!"

Luana Porcello's eyes flew to the Corbetts' front door to see Jenny Corbett storming out with her twin brother, Jimmy, hurrying behind her.

"I tell you, Jen, I didn't do it!" he said.

"And I say you did," Jenny shot back as she ran across their small, picturesque yard with its lush lawn and colorful flower beds.

Jimmy stared after his sister in dismay before trudging toward the sidewalk where Luana stood. His shoulders slumped as he walked, and he stared down at his feet, kicking mildly at the ground. The noonday sunlight glinted gold in his light-brown hair. He was short and skinny and wore thick-rimmed glasses that enlarged his pale-blue eyes to the size of saucers. Something of a junior scientist, Jimmy invariably had an air of distraction about him as he pondered one invention or another.

"Hey, Jimmy, what's up?" Luana watched him with solemn amber eyes.

His head snapped up. "Oh, hi, Luana. I didn't see you standing there." His mouth drooped. "Someone ripped Rebecca's head off, and it's missing. Jenny thinks I did it, but I didn't! She's angry because Mom and Dad believe me and refused to make me pay for it." Rebecca was Jenny's prized Glamor Girl doll and constant companion.

"Oh, that's terrible!" Luana exclaimed. She knew how much Jenny loved her doll. "Who would do such a thing?"

"I don't know." Jimmy released a heavy sigh and ran a hand over his face.

Just then, Jenny stomped up. She was like her twin in appearance—minus the glasses. But in temperament, the two were as different as chalk and cheese because, while Jimmy was quiet and studious, Jenny had a bubbly, outgoing personality, and no one would ever accuse her of being bookish. "What are you doing, Jimmy—confessing your crime to Luana?" she taunted.

"I told you," Jimmy fumed. "I had nothing to do with destroying Rebecca!"

"You're lying!"

"Why are you so determined to believe I broke your doll?"

"Maybe it's because you're always breaking my toys, testing your stupid inventions," said Jenny.

"I admit I've broken some of your toys during my experiments, but that's all in the past. I promised Mom and Dad I wouldn't do that anymore, and I haven't. Besides, I know how much you love Rebecca. I would never hurt her!"

Jenny stuck her nose in the air, folded her

arms, and turned her back to her brother. "I don't believe you!"

Jimmy sighed. "I wish there was some way to prove I didn't hurt your doll."

"And I wish there was a way to prove you did. Then Mom and Dad would make you pay for Rebecca."

Luana stared wide-eyed at the siblings, wringing her hands as she listened to them argue. She was a sweet-natured girl who hated seeing anyone unhappy—especially her friends—and in all the years Luana had known them, she had never seen the twins fight like this. Ordinarily, they were like two peas in a pod. As they continued quarreling, a sudden idea came to her. "Stop fighting, you two. I just thought of a way you can find out what happened to Jenny's doll!"

Jenny and Jimmy turned to stare at her, forgetting their argument for the moment.

"What are you thinking, Luana?" asked Jimmy.

Jenny narrowed her eyes. "Yes, Luana, what *are* you thinking? And why should I trust you? Whatever scheme you have up your sleeve, I'm sure it's for Jimmy's benefit, not mine. You probably believe him and want to prove he's innocent."

"What I believe won't matter," said Luana. "Because my idea is this: we take your case to court!" Her amber eyes sparkled.

"Court!" the twins exclaimed.

"How would we do that?" Jimmy's forehead puckered.

"Yeah," said Jenny. "What court is going to listen to our case?"

Luana beamed. "A kids' court. A court *by* kids *for* kids."

The siblings gaped at her.

"We can have a judge, lawyers, a bailiff—everything just like a real court!" Her face flushed with excitement. "It will be great!"

"I'm not sure." Jimmy massaged the back of his neck.

"Well, my dad says the best way to find the truth is to go to court," said Luana.

The twins looked impressed. All the neighborhood children knew Luana's father was a successful lawyer with the Oakdale District Attorney's Office, working to put bad guys in jail. So, if he said going to court was the best way to find the truth, that was good enough for them.

"OK," said Jenny. "I'm in."

"Me, too." Jimmy nodded. "What do we need to

do?"

"We'll need a few people for my plan to work," said Luana. "Let's get some other kids who want to take part and meet at the fort after lunch. OK?"

"OK," said the twins.

❖ ❖ ❖

Luana bounced into the Porcellos' kitchen. "Hey, Mom."

"Hey, you," her mother said. "Perfect timing. Rosie has lunch ready." Rosie was the family's longtime housekeeper. "What did you do all morning?" Renee Porcello spoke with a mild, lilting Jamaican accent. An attractive woman, she had brown skin, dark, kinky curls, and perceptive dark eyes.

"I hung out at Phoebe's," Luana said, referring to her best friend, Phoebe Chen.

As they were about to sit down to eat a few minutes later, Luana's father strolled into the informal dining room. It was a cozy space separated from the kitchen by a half-wall. The sparse furniture comprised a picnic-style table with benches on either side and a rolling cart in matching oak. Sunlight poured through a large window overlooking the backyard, adding a rosy glow to the room.

"Hey, Dad, what are you doing here?" Luana's lips curved into a broad smile, and the dimples in her cheeks popped.

It was unusual to see David Porcello at home in the middle of the workday. As a senior prosecutor, he had a lot of responsibilities, prosecuting people accused of crimes and supervising a large staff of junior attorneys. "I snuck out of the office to have lunch with my two best girls." He kissed his wife on the cheek. "But shh, it's a secret." His hazel eyes twinkled with mischief as he folded his muscular frame onto the bench next to Luana and tugged one of her long braids.

She giggled.

After saying grace and settling down to eat, Luana told her parents about her plan to start a kids' court.

"That's a great idea, Luana," her father said. "The best way to find the truth is to have an unbiased person review the evidence from both sides." He took a bite out of his turkey sandwich and used a napkin to brush at a few crumbs that clung to his mouth.

"I agree," said her mother. Mrs. Porcello was

also a lawyer but did not work for a government agency as her husband did. Instead, she had a private practice with another attorney.

Luana had spent countless hours at both her parents' offices and in court, observing them while they worked. She found it all very fascinating, so much so that she, too, wanted to be an attorney when she grew up.

"The kids and I are meeting at the fort after lunch," she told her parents. "We need to figure out how to set up the court." She took a sip of lemonade and returned her glass to the table.

"Hmm." David Porcello swallowed a mouthful of chips. "Well, first, you need to decide what type of court you'll have—criminal or civil."

Luana knew criminal courts dealt with cases where people committed crimes. Punishment for those people, if found guilty, included fines and time in jail. Civil courts usually handled cases involving one person suing another for money. "Civil would be best," she said. "We can't exactly put Jimmy in jail, even if he is guilty." She giggled. "Although, I'm sure Jen would love to lock him up and throw away the key if she proves he destroyed Rebecca."

Mrs. Porcello chuckled. "I'm sure she would."

She nibbled on a pickle and thought for a moment. "You'll need a judge and a bailiff." A bailiff was a sheriff's deputy who kept order in the courtroom.

"Plus, an attorney for each side and a court reporter," her father added. It was a court reporter's job to record everything said in court.

"And a jury, of course," said Mrs. Porcello. "Since it's a civil case, you'll need six jurors." A jury was a group of people who listened to the evidence presented in court and decided if the accused person was innocent or guilty.

Luana groaned. That was a lot of people. The neighborhood children were often away at camp or on vacation with their families during the summer. "I don't know if we have that many kids available!"

"What about a bench trial?" her father suggested.

"You mean a trial where the judge listens to both sides and decides if the accused person is innocent or guilty instead of a jury?"

"Exactly!" Mr. Porcello glanced at his watch, then ran his fingers through his dark wavy hair and sighed. "I have to be going. I'm due in court in thirty minutes. Good luck with your court, sweetheart." He gave them each a kiss, then left.

"I have to go too, Mom. I need to make a couple of phone calls before heading to the fort."

"Have fun, dear. I'm meeting with a client at the office this afternoon. You be good for Rosie."

"Aren't I always?" She gave her mother a quick peck on the cheek. "See you later!"

CHAPTER 2

What's My Role?

ON HER WAY to the fort, Luana stopped by Phoebe's house to bring her along to the court meeting. Phoebe lived on the street behind Luana's, and her yard abutted the densely wooded conservation land where the fort was located. Luana told her friend about the kids' court as the two girls walked.

"Oooh, a kids' court is a great idea!" Phoebe's light-brown eyes sparkled.

A large golden retriever went streaking by, carrying a boot in his mouth. He vanished among the trees just as a little boy came running up.

"Have you seen Rufus?" he panted. "He stole my dad's work boot!"

"He ran off that way." Phoebe pointed toward

the trees where the dog had disappeared.

"Thanks." The boy hastened after the animal.

"That dog is a menace!" said Phoebe.

Luana chuckled.

"It's easy for you to laugh." Phoebe huffed. "You don't have to worry about the mangy beast chewing up your stuff. Just last week, he took off with Penelope's flute. I almost had a heart attack!" Her eyes bugged at the memory. "She'd asked me to put it away, and I forgot to do it. I had to chase the wretched beast to the other side of the fort. He was in the middle of digging a hole when I finally caught up to him. Thankfully, I got him before he buried the darn thing, or I'd never have heard the end of it. You know how Penny is about that instrument." Phoebe's sister was an accomplished flutist and had earned a music scholarship to attend college in the coming fall. Her flute was her most prized possession.

Within minutes, the girls arrived at the fort. It was a large clearing enclosed within a circle of tall, heavily branched trees and thick underbrush. Deep in the woods, away from prying parental eyes, it was a popular hangout for each generation of neighborhood kids and had earned the nickname "the fort" years earlier.

Upon their arrival, Luana and Phoebe discovered several friends waiting for them. Besides the Corbett twins, there were three other children: Mary Beth Stover, a pretty blonde whose eyes were so wide set they made one think of a deer in headlights—an image that matched her scatterbrained personality to perfection; Jake Crandall, an overly tall boy whose reddish-blond hair stuck out in every direction; and Lindsey Harrison, a timid girl with dark skin and silver-gray eyes. Ten-year-old Lindsey was a year younger than the others.

As soon as he saw Luana and Phoebe, Jake jumped to his feet. "What's this about you starting a kids' court, Luana?" With his loud voice, massive size, and forceful manner, Jake made for an intimidating presence. However, for all his gruff exterior, he was a sweet kid and a fiercely loyal friend.

"Hello to you, too, Jake." Luana grinned.

He waved off her greeting impatiently.

"I thought it might be a good idea to have a trial to help Jimmy and Jenny figure out what happened to Jenny's doll," she explained.

"What's there to figure out?" He folded his arms across his chest. "Jimmy said he didn't touch her doll. And if Jimmy says he didn't do it, that's good enough for me!"

Jake and Jimmy had been best friends pretty much since birth. They made an odd couple, to be sure. Jimmy was soft-spoken, intelligent, and scholarly, while Jake was loud, did his best to avoid anything to do with books, and wasn't exactly what one would call bright. Nonetheless, Jake's devotion to Jimmy was unswerving, and over the years, he had repeatedly saved his bookish friend from unscrupulous bullies. Everyone at school knew not to mess with Jimmy—not unless they wanted to deal with Jake.

"And I say he did!" Jenny glared at Jake.

"Oh, please," Jake retorted. "You just want Jimmy to pay for your dumb doll. You know he didn't do it."

"I do not!"

Luana rolled her shoulders. Getting this group to settle down and work together would not be easy. She glanced at the sky, admiring the white puffy clouds drifting lazily in the gentle breeze. Then, sighing, she returned her attention to her friends. "Please, guys, let's not argue. The whole reason for starting a court is so we can find the truth without fighting."

"Let's get on with it," said Jimmy. "What do we need to do, Luana?"

"First, we must decide who's going to do what. We need a judge, lawyers for both parties, a bailiff, and a court reporter to start. And we need a jury unless we decide to have a bench trial."

"Can you please speak English?" Jake grumbled. "You lost me. I understand we need a judge and lawyers, but what's this about a party? Will we need music? And what is a bailiff?"

"Not *a* party, Jake," said Luana. "Parties. The parties in a trial are the plaintiff and the defendant. The plaintiff is the person who files the complaint with the court accusing someone of wrongdoing, while the defendant is the person accused." At Jake's blank expression, she sighed again. "In our case, Jenny says Jimmy broke her doll. In court, she is the plaintiff who files the complaint against Jimmy. Jimmy is the defendant—the person accused of destroying the doll."

"So Jenny is a complainer." Jake shrugged. "That's nothing new." Jenny's eyes shot sparks at him, but he ignored her. "And Jimmy is the defendant. I got that, but who are the other people you mentioned, and *what* is a bailiff?"

"A bailiff is a sheriff's deputy who works in a court. He protects the judge and makes sure everyone obeys the court's rules."

"That's me!" Jake thrust his fist in the air. "I'm going to be the bailiff. Do I get to carry a gun? I can bring my MX 5!" The MX 5, a toy gun, was Jake's latest obsession.

"Um, Jake, your MX might be a little on the—the large side. The bailiff carries a—a—a . . ." Luana's voice trailed off.

"What Luana means, Jake, is that the court deputy carries a handgun," said Jimmy.

"Oh." Jake's shoulders sagged, but then he perked up. "So I can't use my MX 5, so what? I get to wear a badge, don't I? I have one that came with the Halloween costume I wore last year." He beamed at the thought.

"Er, sure, Jake," said Luana. "Now for the other people we'll need for the court. We already have our plaintiff and defendant, of course. That's Jenny and Jimmy. We'll need two lawyers, one to represent each of them."

"I'll be Jenny's lawyer," Mary Beth piped up. "I'm sure I can do a good job, Jen," she said to her friend. "You know how obsessed my mom is with those courtroom drama television shows. I watch them with her all the time. Well, the ones she'll let me watch. She says most of them have 'inappropriate content.'" She rolled her blue eyes and made the quotes gesture as she said the words.

Jenny nodded her head in agreement. "Mary Beth is my lawyer."

"I want Luana to be my lawyer," said Jimmy.

"Maybe Luana should be the judge," a quiet voice said. All eyes turned to Lindsey. She had such an unassuming personality that it was often easy to forget she was there. Lindsey's cheeks heated at the children's sudden attention. "After all, a kids' court was her idea," she squeaked. Then she ducked her head, allowing her dark twists to fall forward and hide her face from view.

"Lindsey has a good point," said Phoebe.

"Besides, you're the one who knows the most about courts and legal stuff, Luana. You must have spent half your life at your parents' offices and in real courts!"

"True." Luana bit her lip. "But to be honest, I'd rather be a lawyer. Why don't you be the judge, Lindsey?"

Lindsey's eyes bugged out. "Me? Oh no! I couldn't! I'm not the judge type at all." The others silently agreed. They couldn't imagine the timid Lindsey presiding over a court. "I can be the court reporter," she offered. "I'm a pretty fast typist, and I can record everything on my laptop."

"That would be great, Lindsey." Luana turned to her best friend. "How about you, Pheebs? Any interest in being the judge?"

"Nuh-uh. I'd rather be Jimmy's lawyer."

"OK." Luana wrinkled her nose. "But before I agree to be the judge, let's try to get someone else to do it. We also need a jury, but we might have to do a bench trial."

"There she goes, speaking Greek again," Jake complained. "What is this bench trial you keep talking about? Do we all need to sit on benches or something?"

"No, Jake." Luana laughed. "A bench trial is one

in which the judge decides the outcome."

Jake scratched at his temple. "Huh?"

A corner of her mouth quirked up. "The judge decides who wins. Courts sometimes have bench trials if the parties agree to it. But juries of six or twelve people decide most trials."

"Why can't we have a jury?" Jenny demanded. "Seems to me it would be better to have six people decide instead of one. I mean, that's a lot of power to give one person. And besides, no offense, Luana, but I'm not sure I want *you* making that decision. Everyone knows you have a soft spot for Jimmy."

It was true. Luana had a particular fondness for Jimmy. They shared a mutual love of books and learning and had teamed up on countless school projects.

"The problem is," said Luana, "there aren't that many kids around right now."

"That's true," said Lindsey. "The Hašanis, Newmans, and Castillos are away on vacation."

"Yeah," said Jake, "and the Foster boys and Declan Mathias have day camp all this week."

"That doesn't leave a lot of kids to choose from." Jimmy pushed his glasses up on the bridge of his nose.

"You mean there's no one left," said Phoebe. "Unless you want a jury of four, five, and six-year-olds."

"Absolutely not!" Jenny crossed her arms and stuck out her lower lip. "I don't want a bunch of babies deciding my case."

"Well, that leaves us with only one option," said Luana. "We'll have to have a bench trial."

"What about my sister, Heather?" said Jake. "Maybe we can convince her to be the judge. She's not friends with Jimmy or Jenny, so she wouldn't care who wins. She'll be a pain to put up with, though. Ever since she turned thirteen, she thinks she's soooo cool!" He rolled his eyes.

"Heather is a great idea, Jake!" said Jenny. "We should ask her."

"I agree." Jimmy nodded. "If Heather agrees to be the judge, Luana can be my lawyer."

"OK, great!" Luana's eyes sparkled. "Let's ask her right away so we can get started."

"*Ahem*. Excuse me." Everyone turned to stare at Phoebe. "Haven't you forgotten something?"

"Um, I don't think so." Luana frowned. "*Did* I forget something?"

Phoebe rested a hand on her hip and glowered at her friend. "What about me? Now that you're

Jimmy's lawyer, what part am I going to play in this little courtroom drama, assuming Heather agrees to be the judge?"

"Oh, Pheebs, I'm so sorry!" Luana's hand flew to her open mouth. "Why don't you help me represent Jimmy? You could indulge your Nancy Drew fantasy as his private investigator." She waggled her eyebrows at her friend.

Phoebe's eyes gleamed. There was nothing she liked better than solving puzzles. In this way, she was like her father, Robert Chen, the chief of detectives at the Oakdale Police Department. He often told Phoebe that working on a case was like solving a puzzle. Phoebe thought it would be exciting to solve mysteries, like her father—or Nancy Drew. "Oh, perfect! I've always wanted to be a detective!" She hugged herself.

"Works for me," said Jimmy. "But what exactly will you be doing?"

"Yeah," said Mary Beth. "And how come Jimmy gets to have a private investigator, but Jenny doesn't?"

"Mary Beth's right. It doesn't seem fair," Jenny whined, pouting.

"Let's not argue, guys." Luana bit back yet another sigh. Sweat shone on her golden-brown skin, and she wiped a hand across her forehead. The afternoon sun beat down relentlessly, intensifying the day's heat. "Of course, Jenny can have a private investigator if she wants one. Just find someone who will do it."

"Good. I'll ask Ashley," said Mary Beth, referring to her nine-year-old sister. "She'll do it. She loves watching Mom's court shows almost as much as I do."

"OK, now that's settled, let's go get a judge!" said Phoebe.

CHAPTER 3

You Be the Judge

"WHAT DO YOU children want?" Heather Crandall looked down her nose at her brother and his friends. The group had accosted the teen on the front porch of the Crandall house.

"Um—er—Heath," Jake stammered, "we need a favor."

Heather cocked an eyebrow. "And why would I do anything for you lot?"

"It's like this, Heather," said Luana. "We're starting a kids' court to solve a problem, but we need someone to be the judge."

"Yeah," Phoebe chimed in, "but not just *anyone* can be the judge. The person needs to be firm but fair and highly intelligent. Jake thought you'd be the perfect candidate!" She batted her eyelashes at Heather.

Jake frowned at Phoebe, wondering what on earth she was doing. It looked like she had something in her eye that she was desperately trying to get rid of.

"He did, did he?" Despite her scathing tone, Heather appeared intrigued. "Tell me more about this court and what I would do as the judge. Assuming I agree to do it, of course." She reclined in her chair and folded her hands in her lap, looking at them expectantly.

The children spent the next several minutes telling Heather about the Kids' Court, highlighting how vital the judge's role would be and how ideal she was for the position. There was nothing Heather Crandall enjoyed more than having her ego pampered.

"All right, I'll do it," she announced after they had given her all the details. Her green eyes shone. "When do we start?"

"The sooner, the better," said Luana. "How about tomorrow morning, right after breakfast?"

All the children agreed to the plan.

"But where will we have the court?" asked Lindsey. "We can't exactly do it at the fort. It's a little too uncomfortable, don't you think?"

"Good point, Lindsey." Luana tapped a finger against her right cheek. "Perhaps we can do it in my basement. I'm sure my parents won't mind if we use one of the empty rooms down there."

"Sounds good!" Jake rubbed his hands together. "I can't wait to get started. You all better be on your best behavior, or I'll kick you out of court!"

"Isn't it the judge who decides who gets thrown out of court?" asked Heather.

Jake gave her a disgruntled look. "You aren't going to spend the entire time bossing me around, are you?"

Heather tossed her red hair. "Just make sure you behave, or *I'll* throw *you* out of court!" She smiled at the group, revealing a mouthful of lime-green braces. "I'll see you all tomorrow."

They said their goodbyes and left.

❖ ❖ ❖

The following morning, all the children, including Ashley, who had agreed to be Jenny's private investigator, gathered in the Porcellos' basement. A portion of the area comprised a library, a den, and a workout room. Luana's parents had yet to decide what to do with the rest of the space. One room, intended as a home office for Mrs. Porcello, remained empty, as she had decided she preferred to work in the library or the upstairs study. It was to this room that Luana led the group.

"Mom said we can use this room. She also said we're welcome to any of the old furniture we find stored down here."

"Awesome!" Jake bounced on his toes and swung his arms at his sides as he looked around.

Heather surveyed the space. "It's a perfect size," she said. The room was reasonably large, with several windows and two doors. One door led into the rest of the basement, the other to the outside. The morning sun poured through the windows, giving the room a bright, cheerful atmosphere. "I'm glad we can go in and out without going through the rest of the house. That way, we won't bother your parents with our comings and goings."

Luana chuckled. "Rosie said something about that, too. She's happy we won't be trampling dirt on her clean floors!"

"We should probably get to work, huh?" said Phoebe. "Where's the furniture your parents have stored down here?" She gathered her midnight-black hair into a ponytail and secured it with a yellow scrunchy on top of her head.

"There's a storage room on the other side of the basement," said Luana.

The children headed down the hallway to raid the storage closet. Soon after they got there, Heather claimed an old, battered desk as her own. "This will make a splendid judge's desk, don't you think?" she asked Luana.

"Yeah," Luana agreed. "It's called a bench."

Jake shook his head. "You're losing it, Luana. That is most definitely not a bench. It's a desk."

She laughed. "I didn't mean that, Jake. The desk area where a judge sits in court is called a bench."

"Oh." Jake furrowed his brow. "Why?"

Luana shrugged. "I'm not sure. I guess it's because it's long and resembles a bench, except you sit behind it like a desk instead of on it."

"Well, whatever it's called, I'm taking it for myself." Heather motioned to her brother. "Gimme a hand getting this to the courtroom, will you?" He moved to help her while the other children continued rummaging through the rest of the furniture.

They spent the next hour moving several pieces to the empty room and arranging them to resemble a real court as much as they could. Heather placed her desk at the front, facing the rest of the room, just as a teacher's desk faced her students in a classroom. Lindsey claimed a toddler-sized table with a matching chair as her own. She put them next to Heather's desk at an angle that allowed her to face Heather and the rest of the court. The kids set up two folding tables as counsel desks, one for the defense and one for the plaintiff. They positioned them side-by-side in the middle of the room.

Between the two counsel tables, they settled an old audio-visual cart. Luana thought it was the perfect piece to serve as a lectern, and they could lay their notes and other papers on it while questioning witnesses. The kids took several folding chairs to use as seats and set up a row behind the counsel tables where witnesses and visitors to the court could sit. Jake put his chair on one side of the courtroom where he could, in his words, "keep an eye" on everyone to make sure no one was "causing trouble." While testifying, witnesses would sit in a chair on the opposite side of Heather's desk from Lindsey.

"OK, now that we've got everything where it ought to be, we should probably get started," said

Heather.

"Sounds good," Luana said.

"Wait," said Jake. "Shouldn't Heather have one of those hammer things judges use all the time?"

"Oh, you mean a gavel." Luana considered for a moment. "My dad gave me a toy one a few years ago. I'm sure I still have it somewhere. Wait a sec." She ran out of the room. Several minutes later, she returned, waving a small wooden object in her hand. "Here it is!"

"Thanks." Heather took the wooden toy Luana handed to her. "Before we begin, maybe you could give us a rundown of how we should do things," she suggested.

"That's a good idea," Luana said. "Let me think." She pinched her lower lip. "Well, when we're ready to begin, you say, 'court is in session.' Then, when we're taking a break, you say, 'court is in recess,' and when we're finished for the day, you say, 'court is adjourned.' Because Jenny is the plaintiff, she gets to go first. She has the burden of proof. That means it's her job to convince you Jimmy is guilty. To do that, she must prove her case by a preponderance of the evidence."

"A who of what?" Jake screwed up his face.

"A preponderance of the evidence." Luana

grinned. "It just means she has to prove it's more likely than not Jimmy is guilty. Think of it as a fifty-one, forty-nine percent split. She has to prove it's fifty-one percent likely he's guilty."

"How would she do that?" asked Heather.

"With evidence," said Luana. "She has to bring in evidence that proves her claim against Jimmy. That evidence can be anything, including witness testimony and any items she may have. For example, if she had a picture of Jimmy breaking her doll, she could bring that to court as proof."

"If she had such a picture, we wouldn't need a court, Luana." Ashley giggled. She resembled her sister, with the same honey-blond hair and deep-blue eyes. But where Mary Beth was scatterbrained and indecisive, Ashley was level-headed and resolute.

Luana laughed. "That's true, Ashley."

Jake rubbed his chin. "What's this witness test— test . . . um, what you just said?"

"A witness is someone who gives evidence in court," Luana said. "Witnesses tell what they know about the case. Before they can give evidence, witnesses take an oath promising to tell the truth. The lawyers then ask the witness questions. When the witness speaks or answers questions, it's called testifying."

Luana searched her friends' faces to ensure they understood what she was saying. "In our case, Jenny can bring in witnesses to testify, and she can also testify. When a lawyer questions a witness he brought to court, it's called a direct examination. When the other lawyer questions the witness, it's a cross-examination."

"What about me?" Jimmy asked. "What do I need to do to prove I'm innocent?"

"You don't have to prove you're innocent, Jimmy. The burden of proof is on Jenny. That means it's her job to prove you're guilty. But of course, you can testify, call witnesses, and present evidence that shows you aren't guilty."

"What about the other evidence you mentioned?" asked Heather. "Is there anything special we need to know about them?"

Luana nodded. "Any evidence brought to the court must be authenticated and relevant to the issue. That means a witness must say what it is and explain its importance to the case. The court keeps all the evidence until the trial ends and assigns a letter or number to identify each piece. The labels make it easier for the court to keep track of the various items. In our court, we could label the plaintiff's evidence with letters A, B, C, etcetera, and the defense's with numbers."

"OK, I think we have a good idea of what we're supposed to be doing," said Heather. "What about court rules, Luana? Are there any we should know?"

"Well, there's basic stuff, such as don't interrupt when another person is talking, never argue with the judge, the judge gets the last word, and so on. The court reporter types everything said in court, so only one person should speak at a time. We address the judge as Your Honor, and we should stand when speaking to the court or questioning a witness. When we have anything to say, we say it to the court—the judge being the court. If I have something to say to Mary Beth, I don't speak to her directly but speak to Heather—the court. And to keep things formal, we shouldn't use our first names."

Mary Beth blinked. "But if we don't use our first names, what are we supposed to call each other?"

Phoebe facepalmed. "We have last names."

"Oh, yes. Yes, of course." Mary Beth chewed her lower lip.

"What's the matter, Mary Beth?" Heather

asked, noticing the worried expression on her face.

"I was just wondering how I'll keep track of all the names. I mean, first names, last names—that's a lot of names!" Mary Beth's eyebrows drew together as she stared at her friends. "Don't you think?"

Phoebe gave an exaggerated sigh.

"Maybe we can just put miss or mister before our first names," Lindsey suggested. "For instance, I'd be Miss Lindsey."

"That's a great idea, Lindsey!" Ashley said.

The others agreed.

"Is there anything else, Luana?" Heather asked.

"No, I think that's it."

"All right, then." Heather clapped her hands. "Let's get started. Mary Beth, as Jenny's lawyer, you get to go first. Are you ready?"

"Yes, we're ready," said Mary Beth.

"OK, everyone, the Kids' Court is now in session." Heather banged the gavel on her desk.

Ashley tittered, earning herself a warning glance from Heather.

"The case we're here to decide is Jenny Corbett versus Jimmy Corbett," said Heather. "Miss Jenny claims Mr. Jimmy destroyed her Glamor Girl doll.

Mr. Jimmy denies her charge. Miss Mary Beth, you may begin."

Mary Beth jumped to her feet and trotted to the makeshift lectern. "Thank you, Your Honor. Jenny—I mean, Miss Jenny—will be my first witness."

"Please come forward, Miss Jenny, and sit in the witness chair." Heather pointed to the chair on her left. "Deputy Jake, please swear in the witness."

Jake swaggered forward, puffing out his chest to show off the shiny, metallic sheriff's badge he wore. "Please raise your right hand."

Jenny raised her hand.

"Do you promise to tell the truth, the whole truth, and nothing but the truth?"

"I do."

"Thank you, Deputy Jake," said Heather. "You may begin, Miss Mary Beth."

"Miss Jenny, do you know the, er . . . ?" Mary Beth's voice trailed off. "Um, Luana, what's Jimmy called again?"

"Huh?" Luana furrowed her brow. "I'm sorry, Mary Beth. I'm not sure what you're asking."

"Sorry," said Mary Beth. "Jenny says Jimmy ruined her doll. So that makes him the . . . ?"

"Oh, I see," said Luana. "Jimmy is the defendant."

"Oh yes, that's it. Thanks." Mary Beth beamed. "Miss Jenny, do you know the defendant, Jimmy Corbett?"

"Yes, I do."

"How is it you know him?"

"He's my brother."

"Um, how long have you known him?"

"All my life."

"All your life." Mary Beth paused. "And, er . . . how—how long has that been?"

"I'm eleven, so I've known him for eleven years."

"Um, do you—do you live together?"

"Yes, we do," said Jenny.

Next to Luana, Phoebe fidgeted in her chair.

"And—and how long have you—er, lived together?" asked Mary Beth.

"All our lives."

"I . . . see." Mary Beth chewed her lower lip.

"Um . . . ah." She paused. "How—how long has that been?"

Jenny frowned. "Eleven years."

Phoebe smothered a laugh, and Luana nudged her in the side, signaling her to be quiet.

Phoebe crossed her eyes at Luana, then returned her attention to Mary Beth, who leaned against the lectern with a glazed expression in her eyes—the minutes ticked by as she stared into space.

Finally, Heather broke the silence. "Miss Mary Beth, are you finished?"

"Huh?" Mary Beth started. "Um, no, Heather—I mean, Your Honor. I'm sorry, I was trying to gather my thoughts." She blinked. "I'm ready with my next question."

"That's good," said Heather. "Go ahead."

Mary Beth wiped her sweaty palms on her pink t-shirt. "Jenny—er, Miss Jenny, how—how long, um, how long has the defendant known you?"

Unable to control herself any longer, Phoebe burst out laughing. Mary Beth's face turned beet-red as she whirled to face Phoebe, planting her hands on her hips. "Phoebe Chen, you stop laughing this instant! I'd like to see you try to do this."

"I'm sorry! I'm sorry!" Phoebe gasped. She bent her head over her knees and laughed even harder.

"Order in the court!" Heather repeatedly thumped the gavel on her desk. "Phoebe Chen, pull yourself together, or I'll have the bailiff remove you from my courtroom!"

"I'm sorry, Your Honor," Phoebe spluttered. She covered her mouth with both hands, trying to stifle her laughter.

"This is harder than it looks on TV." Mary Beth huffed. "I'm not even sure what I'm supposed to be asking."

"You're right, Mary Beth," said Luana. "It is a lot harder than it looks. And as the plaintiff's lawyer, you have the difficult task of proving Jenny's case against Jimmy."

"How do I do that?" asked Mary Beth.

"Well, I think you got off to a great start." Luana gave her an encouraging smile. "You showed the relationship between Jenny and Jimmy, which is important. Now, you need to prove the main parts of your case: Jenny owns a Glamor Girl doll, someone destroyed the doll, and Jimmy is the person who destroyed it.

"You'll need to bring in evidence, such as Jenny's testimony, any witnesses you may have, and any other proof. It might help if you wrote out your questions, or at least a few notes, to remind yourself of the main points you want to bring out when you question each witness."

Mary Beth nodded her head. "I think I've got it." She bit her lower lip. "Would it be possible to take a break so I can prepare a little, Heather? I know I said I was ready, but that was before I realized how much I have to do."

Heather frowned. "OK, but make sure you're actually ready to begin when we come back."

Two spots of pink appeared on Mary Beth's cheeks. "Yes, Your Honor," she mumbled. "I'll be ready."

"I hope so," said Heather. "All right, we'll break now and come back after lunch. Does that work for everyone?"

All the children agreed to the plan.

"Very well." Heather banged the gavel. "The court is in recess."

CHAPTER 4

The Drama Begins

"HOW'S COURT GOING?" asked Rosie as Luana and Phoebe came scuttling into the kitchen. The room was large, warm, and welcoming, much like the woman who presided over it. A gentle breeze entered through the open windows, and the delicious scent of roasted chicken wafted throughout, causing the girls' mouths to water.

"Good," said Luana.

Phoebe snickered. "We didn't get very far. We ran into some unexpected difficulties."

Rosalie McDonald raised her eyebrows in question. She was an imposing woman with dark skin and intelligent brown eyes. Like Luana's mother, she was a Jamaican native and spoke with an accent much heavier than Mrs. Porcello's.

Luana gave Rosie a rueful smile. "Mary Beth was a little confused about what to do. She wasn't sure how to go about proving Jenny's claim."

Rosie was intimately familiar with the case; Luana had regaled her with all the details the previous evening. "I'm sure you helped her figure things out," she said to Luana.

"Yes, she did," said Phoebe. "But then Mary Beth asked for a break to prepare. We're meeting up again after lunch." She licked her lips. "Speaking of lunch, Rosie, the chicken smells heavenly. Is there any chance we could have some of it? Please?"

"Coming right up." Rosie moved around the kitchen, preparing chicken sandwiches for the girls' meal.

While they ate, Phoebe and Luana discussed the case.

"How do you think Mary Beth will prove Jimmy broke Jenny's doll?" asked Phoebe, taking a bite out of her sandwich.

"I'm not sure." Luana twirled a dark braid around her finger. "I've been racking my brain all night wondering about that. It's not like Jenny saw him do it. Otherwise, she would have told her parents."

"That's true." The two friends descended into silence as they concentrated on their food.

After a short while, Luana took a swallow of apple juice, washing down the last of her sandwich. "However they go about proving it, we need to prepare ourselves," she said, finally breaking the silence.

"Yeah." Phoebe chomped on a pickle. "Knowing Mary Beth, this trial could easily turn into an episode of one of her beloved court shows." She shook her head. "We'd better be ready for anything."

❖ ❖ ❖

Mary Beth returned to court that afternoon, lugging a heavy-looking cardboard box in her arms.

"What's that?" Phoebe asked.

"You'll see." Mary Beth's blue eyes twinkled.

Phoebe and Luana exchanged glances. They wondered what trick Mary Beth had up her sleeve.

When Heather arrived, she immediately got down to business. "Order in the court." She banged the gavel. "Is everyone here?"

"We're all here, Your Honor," said Luana.

"Good, then let's get started." Heather banged the gavel again. "The court is now in session. Miss Mary Beth, are you ready to begin?"

"Yes, Your Honor."

Jenny returned to the witness chair.

"Remember, Miss Jenny, you're still under oath," said Heather.

"Yes, Your Honor."

"Miss Jenny," said Mary Beth, "you've accused your brother, Jimmy, of destroying your Glamor Girl doll. Has he ever broken any of your other toys?"

"Yes, lots of times." Jenny clenched her jaw.

"Tell us about some of those times."

"Jimmy fancies himself an inventor. He's always coming up with new ideas, and then he has to test them to see if they work." Jenny made a sour face. "One time, he built this—this . . . this *thing*. He said it was a rocket, but it didn't look like any rocket *I'd* ever seen. Anyway, he claimed he could use it to send objects to the moon."

"Did he ever test it to see if it would work?"

"Yes."

"What did he try to send to the moon?"

"He tried to send Ellie. She is—or, rather, she *was*—my stuffed elephant." Jenny's mouth set in a hard line.

"Why do you say she *was* your stuffed elephant?" asked Mary Beth.

"Because his stupid invention didn't work!" Jenny scowled. "He strapped my poor Ellie to his so-called rocket, but when he tried to launch it, it exploded and blew Ellie to bits! Her stuffing flew everywhere." Tears sprang to her eyes.

Next to Luana, Jimmy squirmed in his seat. "I said I was sorry, Jen. I never meant to hurt Ellie. I was sure my rocket would work!"

"Silence, Mr. Jimmy," Heather barked. She emphasized her order by rapping the gavel on her desk. "You may continue, Miss Mary Beth."

Ashley gave a slight shake of her head. Heather sure loved banging that gavel.

"Thank you, Your Honor." Mary Beth's

expression softened. "Miss Jenny, I know it must be dreadfully painful for you to relive this horrible event, but I need to ask you a few more questions."

"That's fine." Jenny sniffled and blew her nose into a tissue she had pulled from her pocket. "I can continue."

Jake mentally rolled his eyes. He couldn't believe the fuss Jenny was making over some old stuffed animal. Girls were so dumb.

Reaching into the cardboard box she had brought to court, Mary Beth pulled out a small wooden box. "Your Honor, I'd like to have this item identified as plaintiff's A."

"The court will identify it as plaintiff's A in the record," said Heather.

Mary Beth held up the wooden box. "Miss Jenny, I am showing you what the court has identified as plaintiff's A. Do you recognize it?"

Jenny nodded. "I do."

"Please tell the court what it is."

"It's the box in which I keep Ellie."

"I'm sorry, didn't you say your brother blew Ellie to bits?"

"He did, but I collected all the pieces I could find and put them in that box. Ellie was my best friend for nine years! I couldn't just throw her away!" Jenny pulled out a clean tissue and dabbed at her eyes.

Mary Beth approached Jenny and handed her the box. "Can you please open the wooden box I just gave you and show the court what's inside?"

Jenny did as she was told. She turned the box around so the others could see its contents. Inside was a mass of white substance that looked almost exactly like cotton balls. Scattered throughout were little pieces of light-gray material.

Busy typing on her computer, Lindsey raised her eyes to Heather, frowning. "I'm not sure how I'm supposed to record what's in the box."

"Good point, Lindsey," said Heather. "Any ideas, Luana—I mean, Miss Luana?"

"You could have the witness describe the contents, Your Honor," said Luana.

Heather nodded. "That sounds like a good idea. Miss Jenny, please describe the contents of the box."

"Um, it's a lot of white cotton batting," said Jenny. "My mom told me that's what they called the material they used to stuff toys long ago. Ellie was ancient. She belonged to my grandmother, my mother, then me. Now she's gone forever! And it's all his fault!" She extended her right arm and pointed a finger at Jimmy as a tear rolled down her cheek.

Heather rolled her eyes. "Pull yourself together, Miss Jenny. Miss Mary Beth, do you have any more questions for this witness?"

"Yes, I do, Your Honor."

"Well, please continue."

"Miss Jenny, tell us about another time when your brother destroyed one of your toys," said Mary Beth.

"There was the time he cut off Miss Pig Pen's leg when he tried to invent a pair of baby-safe scissors. Our brother, Colin, was a baby then and always wanted to play with them. He would cry for the scissors whenever Jimmy or I used them. Jimmy tried to blunt the edges of a pair to make them safe for Colin to play with. *That* didn't work, and when he cut Miss Pig Pen's leg to show how safe they were, he cut it off!"

Mary Beth again reached into the cardboard box and pulled out a toy pig, missing its right leg from just below the knee. "Your Honor, can we label this item plaintiff's B for identification?"

"Yes, we will identify it as plaintiff's B," said Heather.

"Is this Miss Pig Pen?" Mary Beth asked Jenny. Jenny nodded. "Yes."

"Yikes! That's a nasty cut," said Heather. "Lindsey, the doll has its right leg removed below the knee. Perhaps you should type that in the record." She glanced at Luana. "We should have a record of what the toy looks like, right?"

"Yes, we should," Luana agreed.

"Go ahead, Miss Mary Beth," said Heather after Lindsey finished typing the toy's description.

"Thank you, Your Honor."

For the next half an hour, Jenny recited experiment after experiment by which Jimmy had destroyed one toy or another. With each recitation, Mary Beth produced the mangled remains of the toy, and Jenny described each one for the court record. Lindsey dutifully typed everything on her laptop.

Phoebe sighed and leaned in closer to Luana. "How much longer is this memorial to Jenny's toys going to continue?" she whispered.

Luana shrugged, a smile tugging at her lips. Patience was not one of Phoebe's virtues. To Phoebe's relief, Mary Beth started asking Jenny about the events leading up to Rebecca's destruction a few minutes later.

"Miss Jenny, let us talk about the day you found your Glamor Girl doll, Rebecca, beheaded. Did you see Jimmy break your doll?"

"No, I did not."

"Then why do you think he's the one who broke it?"

"I don't *think* he broke my doll. I *know* he did!"

"Please tell the court how you came to that conclusion," said Mary Beth.

"That morning, I was playing with Rebecca in the backyard. We were having a tea party." Jenny drew in a shaky breath. "Rebecca loved tea parties." Her voice quivered.

Heather sighed to herself. All this drama over a doll was beyond ridiculous. *Children*, she thought, curling her upper lip.

"Anyway, there's a shed in the backyard where Jimmy creates his inventions." Jenny sneered. "He says it's his laboratory, but it's just an old shed Dad no longer uses. He lets Jimmy use it to store all his garbage."

"It's not garbage!" Jimmy burst out. "Those are all my scientific equipment."

"Mr. Jimmy." Heather banged the gavel. "Be quiet."

Jenny smirked at Jimmy. "He says scientific

equipment; I say garbage. Whatever you want to call it, Jimmy keeps it in the shed. While Rebecca and I were having our tea party, Jimmy came out of the shed. He was working on another of his inventions—a glue he said would bond any material. When he came out, he asked if I had any broken toys that needed fixing. He said he wanted to test his glue. I told him I didn't have any and to stay away from my toys. He returned to the shed, muttering about needing to break something so he could fix it. Then Mom called me inside." She paused and looked at Mary Beth in question, unsure if she should continue.

Mary Beth inclined her head. "Go on. What happened next?"

"When I went to see what Mom wanted, she asked me to return a baking pan to Mrs. Cuthbert. She had given us a pie a few days earlier. On the way back from Mrs. Cuthbert, I saw you, Mary Beth, and we went to your house to watch a movie. I didn't remember to go back to get Rebecca until later that night. When I did, I found her headless body lying on the ground outside the shed door. I searched the entire yard but couldn't find her head anywhere." Jenny's eyes impaled her brother. "I know he broke my doll. He needed a broken toy to test his dumb glue, and when he couldn't find one, he destroyed my Rebecca!"

Mary Beth reached into the cardboard box yet again. It surprised no one when she produced the headless body of a Glamor Girl doll. She held up the toy. "Is this Rebecca?"

"Yes, that's her," whispered Jenny. More tears rolled down her cheeks, and she lowered her gaze to her lap, where she twisted her hands together.

"For the record, Your Honor, I am showing the headless body of a Glamor Girl doll to Miss Jenny. If it pleases the court, may we label it plaintiff's K for identification?"

"The court will label the doll as plaintiff's K in the record," said Heather. "Do you have any more questions for this witness?"

"No, Your Honor. I'm finished with my direct examination."

"Miss Luana, do you have questions for Miss Jenny?" asked Heather.

"Yes, I do, Your Honor."

Phoebe grabbed her arm as Luana was about to move to the lectern. "Ask for a quick break," she hissed. At Luana's puzzled expression, she explained, "I want to examine the doll."

Luana nodded. "Your Honor, I would like to

request a brief recess."

"OK." Heather glanced at her watch. "It's kinda late. Why don't we just adjourn until tomorrow morning?"

"That's fine, Your Honor," said Luana. "My investigator would like to examine plaintiff's K. Can you ask the bailiff to remain behind for a few minutes?" They had decided that Jake should be in charge of the evidence.

"Sure thing," said Heather. "Deputy Jake, allow Miss Phoebe a few minutes to examine plaintiff's K."

"Huh?" Jake gave his sister a blank look.

Heather pinched the bridge of her nose. "Phoebe wants to look at the doll—the headless one."

"Oh. Why didn't you just say so?" said Jake.

"I just did," she snapped. "Is there anything else we need to deal with before we break for the day?" Heather's eyes swept over the group, and after they assured her there was nothing, she banged the gavel. "Court is adjourned."

CHAPTER 5

Crossing Jenny

LUANA, PHOEBE, AND Jimmy gazed at the doll Jake had given them a few minutes earlier. Jake had written the letter K on tape and stuck it to the doll's leg.

"What are you looking for, Pheebs?" asked Luana.

"Clues." Phoebe turned over the doll she held in her hands.

Luana and Jimmy exchanged glances.

"What clues?" said Jimmy.

"I'll know when I find them." Phoebe retrieved a magnifying glass from her mini backpack and examined the doll through the lens. "There are several small dents on the doll's body," she said as she removed pieces of its clothing.

Jimmy and Luana inched closer to peer at the doll.

"Yes, I see them." Jimmy blinked. "And there's a small hole in the stomach. I wonder how that happened."

"I don't know." A line etched between Phoebe's brows. "That's what Luana will have to find out when she questions Jenny." She inspected the doll's severed neck, running her fingers around the edges. "Someone ripped the head off this thing. The edges are all jagged."

Luana played with one of her dark braids for a few moments, deep in thought, then awe transformed her face. "You're quite the investigator, Pheebs! You've given me a direction for my cross-examination tomorrow."

❖ ❖ ❖

As soon as Heather declared the court in session the following morning, Luana began her cross-examination. "Good morning, Miss Jenny."

"Good morning," said Jenny.

"Yesterday, you recited a long list of incidents where Jimmy destroyed several of your toys while testing his various inventions."

"Yes, I did, and that wasn't the half of it."

"Yes, but in any of those many instances, did he ever deny causing the damage to the toy?"

"Well, n—no," said Jenny.

"So, in all the years he's been destroying your toys, he's never once denied breaking one when he did?"

Jenny's pale-blue eyes flashed. "I know what you're trying to do, Luana Porcello, and I don't like it! For your information, he broke those other toys before Mom and Dad told him he'd have to pay to replace any he destroyed, and none of them were as expensive as Rebecca."

Luana ignored Jenny's outburst. "Was there a witness every time he broke a toy?"

"No, there wasn't."

"And when he broke toys, and no one saw him do it, how did you know Jimmy had broken them?"

Jenny's jaw tightened. She said nothing.

"Your Honor, would you please instruct the witness to answer the question?" said Luana.

"Miss Jenny, answer the question, or I'll find you in contempt of court." Since becoming the judge, Heather spent a lot of time researching court procedures on the internet.

Jenny stuck out her lower lip. "What was the question again?"

Luana repeated her question. "When he broke toys, and no one saw him do it, how did you know Jimmy had broken them?"

Jenny huffed. "He would admit it."

"He didn't admit to ruining Rebecca, did he?"

"No, he didn't. He said he didn't do it. But Rebecca is way more expensive than any other toy he's broken in the past."

"Your Honor, may I have plaintiff's K to ask the witness a few questions about it?" said Luana.

"Yes, of course, Miss Luana," Heather said. "Deputy Jake, please give Counsel plaintiff's K."

Jake's mouth fell open. "Give what to who?"

Heather gritted her teeth. "Counsel—Miss Luana. Please give her plaintiff's K—the headless doll."

"Why couldn't you just say that?" Jimmy

grumbled. Ever since his sister had become the judge, she was even more impossible to deal with than ever. He removed Rebecca from the box where the evidence was stored and gave the doll to Luana.

Luana held up the toy. "Miss Jenny, is this exactly how your doll looked when you found her lying on the ground outside the shed?"

"Yes, it is."

"You haven't washed her, changed her clothes, or done anything else since you found her?" asked Luana, raising her eyebrows.

"Well, I washed her. She was all wet and covered with some kind of . . . I don't know, a kind of sticky substance." Jenny's eyes shot daggers at her brother. "I'm sure it was Jimmy's glue."

Luana glanced at the doll. She frowned. *A sticky substance? Could it have been Jimmy's glue?* "What color was this sticky substance?"

"It didn't have a color. I couldn't see it; I just felt it."

"What about her clothes? Are these the ones she was wearing on the day in question?"

"No, I changed her clothes. The ones she wore were all dirty, and there was a rip in her shirt."

"OK. Now, Miss Jenny, I'd like you to look

closely at Rebecca's body." Luana crossed the distance to Jenny and handed her the doll. "Please describe what you see."

"There are little dent marks all over her chest, tummy, and legs, and she has a small hole in her stomach." Jenny released a shuddering breath.

"Were these marks on Rebecca before you found her lying on the ground?"

"No, absolutely not!" Jenny's brows snapped together. "Rebecca was in perfect condition. There wasn't a scratch on her."

"Thank you, Miss Jenny. Your Honor, I have no further questions for this witness."

"Excellent!" said Heather. "Miss Mary Beth, do you have any other witnesses to call?"

"I do, Your Honor, but unfortunately, he's at day camp and won't be available until later this afternoon," Mary Beth replied. "If it would be OK, can we take a break until then?"

Heather raised her eyebrows. "Just who is this witness?"

"It's Declan Mathias, Your Honor."

Declan Mathias? What could he possibly know about the case? Luana wondered.

"Do you have other witnesses or evidence to present to the court in the meantime?" Heather asked. "I hate to waste an entire afternoon just waiting around." She had read judges did not like wasting their courts' time.

"No, Your Honor, I don't." Mary Beth wiped sweaty palms on her t-shirt and cleared her throat. "Declan should be available around three-thirty."

"Miss Luana, do you have anything to say about this?" asked Heather.

"The court could ask Miss Mary Beth to give a proffer," Luana suggested.

"Huh?" Heather tilted her head to one side and scrunched up her face. "What's that?"

"What I mean is, you could ask Miss Mary Beth to give an offer of proof; ask her to tell the court what she expects Mr. Declan to say in his testimony," said Luana. "To my knowledge, Declan knows nothing about the destruction of Jenny's doll."

"Excellent point, Miss Luana. What about it, Miss Mary Beth? What exactly is your reason for calling Declan to testify?"

"He's an eyewitness, Your Honor."

"An eyewitness!" Luana, Phoebe, and Jimmy exclaimed, their faces mirroring similar expressions of surprise.

"What's this all about?" Phoebe muttered to the other two.

"I don't know," Luana whispered back. "Do you know anything about this, Jimmy?"

"No." Jimmy's face wore a blank expression. "I don't know what Declan could have seen. I never touched Rebecca!"

"Well, we'll find out soon enough, I suppose." Luana wrinkled her nose. She didn't like surprises.

"If there are no objections, I will adjourn court until this afternoon. We will meet back here at three-thirty." Heather banged the gavel. "The court is in recess."

CHAPTER 6

Caught in the Act

THAT AFTERNOON, THE children sat around munching on a tray of goodies Rosie had brought downstairs.

"Mmm! These cookies are delicious!" Phoebe took a giant bite out of her chocolate chip cookie.

"Yeah." Jake licked his lips. "Rosie makes the best cookies!"

"I have to agree with you, dweeb boy. These are fantastic." Heather nibbled on a sugar cookie.

"I like the brownies best." Lindsey's mouth curved into a broad smile as she reached for a second chocolate chip brownie.

Just then, Mary Beth, Jenny, and Ashley entered the courtroom. A brown-skinned boy of average height accompanied them. It was Declan

Mathias, the twins' next-door neighbor.

"Hey, Dec Man," Jake greeted him.

"Hey, Jake," said Declan. "I hear you guys started a court. That's pretty cool!"

"Yeah." Jake stuck out his chest, showing off the costume sheriff's badge he wore. "I'm the Kids' Court deputy."

Heather rolled her eyes at her brother's boasting. "Hi, Declan." She moved to her desk. "Let's get started, everyone. It's getting late." After they all took their seats, she declared the court in session. "Mr. Declan, you stand here to be sworn in, then you may sit down." She pointed to a spot in front of the witness chair. "Bailiff, you may give the oath to the witness."

Jake strutted forward. "Please raise your right hand."

Declan raised his hand.

"Do you promise to tell the truth, the whole truth, and nothing but the truth?"

"I do."

"Thank you, Deputy Jake," Heather said. "Mr. Declan, you may sit. Miss Mary Beth, you may begin."

"Good afternoon, Mr. Declan," said Mary Beth.

Declan's mouth twitched. "Good afternoon,

Miss Mary Beth."

"Mr. Declan, do you know my client, Jenny Corbett?"

"Yes, I do. She's my next-door neighbor."

"So you also know her brother, Jimmy?"

"Yes."

"How long have you known the Corbetts?"

"Six years. I met them when my family moved here."

"Would you say you and the Corbetts are friends?" asked Mary Beth.

"I'd say we're more friendly than friends. They're a couple of years behind me in school." Declan relaxed in his chair.

"OK. Now, Mr. Declan, let's talk about July fifth, the day Jenny found her doll beheaded. Where were you that afternoon?"

"I was at home."

"Did you see Jimmy?"

"Yes, I did."

"When was that?"

"It was just about one o'clock. I looked out my bedroom window and saw Jimmy standing in his backyard."

"What was he doing?"

"He had a toy in one hand. It looked like a doll.

In his other hand, he held an ax."

Luana stiffened. *Jimmy had an ax?*

"An ax?" Mary Beth said. "Did you see what he did with it?"

"Yes. He put the toy on the chopping block, then used the ax to cut it in half. He took one swing, and the two pieces flew in opposite directions." Declan moved his arms to simulate a chopping motion. "It was pretty cool!"

Loud gasps emitted throughout the courtroom as the children reacted to the news Jimmy had destroyed a doll.

Oh, no! Goosebumps rose on Luana's skin. Jimmy had chopped a doll in two. Had it been Rebecca? She glanced at Jimmy, who sat beside her, staring unblinkingly at Declan. She noticed he looked pale, and beads of sweat clung to his forehead. *Is he guilty?* she wondered.

"You're sure this happened three days ago, on the afternoon of July fifth?" Mary Beth leaned against the lectern, resting her forearms on its surface.

"Yes, I'm sure. It was Sunday afternoon. I remember because the day before was the fourth. Besides, I have baseball camp every day during the week, and on Saturdays, I have soccer practice from eleven to two. Sundays are the only day I'm at home for lunch. And I remember the time exactly because Mom had just called me downstairs to eat. You can set your watch by Mom's mealtimes on the weekends. Breakfast at nine, lunch at one, dinner at five-thirty—it never changes."

"Thank you, Mr. Declan," said Mary Beth. "I have no more questions for Mr. Declan, Your Honor."

"Excellent!" Heather's face beamed. "Things are moving along at a splendid pace. Miss Luana, I assume you'd like to ask Mr. Declan a few questions?"

"Yes, Your Honor, I would," said Luana. "But may I have a short recess to prepare my cross-examination?"

Heather pressed her lips together. "How much time are we talking about, Miss Luana? I want to get this done today. You heard Declan; he has camp five days a week. If you don't finish your cross-examination today, we'll have to waste all day tomorrow waiting for him to come home."

"I'm sorry, Your Honor. I really need a break. It can be a short one."

"Very well." Heather sighed and banged the

gavel. "Court is in recess for fifteen minutes." She scowled at Luana. "That enough time for you?"

"Yes, thank you, Your Honor. Fifteen minutes is perfect."

❖ ❖ ❖

"What was all that about?" Phoebe's eyes emitted gold sparks as she marched back and forth, her bone-straight hair whipping about her head. She stopped in front of Jimmy, eyeing him balefully.

She, Jimmy, and Luana were in the Porcellos' kitchen. The other children were downstairs finishing Rosie's treats.

"You said you didn't destroy Rebecca!" Phoebe resumed pacing.

"I didn't!" Jimmy ran a hand through his hair.

Phoebe turned to glare at him. "Then what about Declan seeing you hack a doll into pieces?"

"He must have seen me when I cut Kid in two," Jimmy mused.

"What?" said Luana. "Who's Kid?"

"My Kid Kenny doll. I needed a broken toy I could use to test my glue. I couldn't find any, so I had to break one."

"So you chopped your Kid Kenny in half?"

Phoebe's mouth fell open.

"Yes. I don't play with it anymore." Jimmy shrugged. "I figured it wouldn't matter if my glue didn't work and I couldn't fix it."

"Why didn't you tell us about this from the beginning, Jimmy?" asked Luana.

"I didn't think it was important. The issue is whether I broke Rebecca, and I didn't."

"I know, but now we have an eyewitness who just testified he saw you take an ax to a toy—a *doll*—on the very day someone ripped the head off Jenny's doll!" Luana twisted a braid around her finger. "Perhaps if you'd thought to mention this before, we could have prepared for this possibility." She released a heavy breath. "We'd better come up with a plan."

❖ ❖ ❖

Several minutes later, the trio returned to the courtroom armed with a plan of action. As soon as Heather saw them approaching, she sat at her bench and banged the gavel. "Court is now in session. Miss Luana, I assume you're ready to begin?"

"I am, Your Honor. With the court's permission, I'd like to do my cross-examination at the scene."

"What?" Heather's brows snapped together. "What are you saying, Luana?"

"I'm sorry, Your Honor. What I mean is, I'd like to question Mr. Declan in his room—the place where he said he was when he saw my client."

"Er—OK," said Heather. "That OK with you, Declan?"

Declan shrugged. "Sure."

"All right then, let's go, everyone. We're taking the court on the road!" said Heather. They all filed out of the courtroom a few minutes later, heading to Declan's house.

❖ ❖ ❖

The children soon arrived at Declan's residence and headed upstairs to his room. It was neat, with a queen-sized bed, a dresser, and a desk. Shelves stuffed with various athletic trophies and sports memorabilia lined one wall.

As soon as they had settled, Luana began her cross-examination. "Mr. Declan, you testified you were at home in this room on the afternoon of July fifth. Is that correct?"

"That's right," said Declan.

"You said you saw Jimmy in his backyard

around one o'clock?"

"Yes, I did. I saw him from my bedroom window."

Luana walked to the window and gazed outside. "Please show the court exactly where you saw Jimmy."

Declan moved to stand next to Luana. All the children except Lindsey followed. She was sitting at Declan's desk, typing on her laptop. He  pointed out the window toward Jimmy's backyard. "He was standing right there, exactly where Phoebe is now."

"Hey," Ashley cried, "why is Phoebe in Jenny's backyard?"

"Quiet!" Heather's eyes combed the area, looking for somewhere to bang her gavel. She finally settled on the windowsill, rapping the hammer several times in a row.

Jake made a slight sound of disgust. His sister was on a major power trip.

"Please continue, Miss Luana," said Heather.

"I asked Phoebe to go over there. It will help during my cross-examination." Pulling her cell phone from a pocket, Luana sent Phoebe a text. "Mr. Declan, you said you saw Jimmy standing where Phoebe is now around one o'clock on the fifth. Is that correct?"

"Yes." Declan nodded.

"For the record, Your Honor, Phoebe is standing in the Corbetts' backyard next to a chopping block," said Luana.

"So noted in the record," Heather said.

"Mr. Declan, is Phoebe holding anything in her hands?" Luana stared out the window as she asked the question.

Declan gazed out the window at Phoebe. "Yes, she's holding a toy. A doll, I think."

"Do you know what type of doll she's holding?"

Declan leaned closer to the window and squinted. Finally, he shook his head. "N–no."

"Does it resemble the toy you saw Jimmy holding Sunday afternoon?"

"Yes, it's pretty similar."

"Would you say it's the same toy?" asked Luana.

"It could be. I'm not sure." Declan rested his

hands on the windowsill and pressed his forehead against the glass. "Honestly, I wasn't paying too much attention to the toy. I just know it was some kind of doll."

"Thank you, Mr. Declan. Your Honor, I have no further questions for this witness."

"Excellent!" said Heather. "Miss Mary Beth, will you be calling any other witnesses?"

"No, Your Honor," said Mary Beth. "The plaintiff rests."

"You're tired?" Jake gawked at Mary Beth.

"No, Jake." Luana laughed. "Mary Beth means she's finished with her case. She has no more witnesses or evidence to bring to court."

"If you've finished with the vocabulary lesson," said Heather, "let's get on with it. Will you be ready to begin your case in the morning, Luana?"

"Yes, Your Honor, I'll be ready."

"Very good." Heather banged the gavel. "Court is adjourned until tomorrow morning."

CHAPTER 7

Jimmy Comes Clean

LUANA LAY IN bed, staring at the ceiling. Jimmy's case preoccupied her mind. *Is he as innocent as he claims he is? Maybe he isn't telling the truth. He does have a perfect reason to lie—Glamor Girl dolls are super expensive. And what about that sticky substance Jenny said she noticed on Rebecca? Could that have been Jimmy's glue?*

There was a quiet knock at the bedroom door before Renee Porcello peeked in. "May I come in?"

Luana greeted her mother with a smile. "Of course."

"I came to tuck you in."

Luana rolled her eyes. "I'm not a baby, Mom," she protested. "I'll be eleven in less than a month!"

"You'll always be *my* baby." Mrs. Porcello

clucked her tongue as she smoothed down Luana's sheets. "What's wrong?"

"What makes you think anything is wrong?"

"You only pull your hair when you're upset, anxious, or preoccupied." Her mother sat on the edge of the bed and pointed to the braid wrapped around Luana's finger. "You're about to twist that braid right off your head."

Luana looked at the hair she held and grimaced, noticing its mangled appearance. Sighing, she dropped it. "Nothing's wrong. Not really. I was just thinking. Mary Beth finished Jenny's case today, so it's my turn to present Jimmy's side. I've been trying to think of a way to prove he's innocent."

"Well, that's your first mistake."

"What do you mean?"

"You forget one of the fundamental principles of law," her mother said. "It's the plaintiff's responsibility to prove the defendant's guilt, not the defendant's job to prove his innocence."

"You're right, of course. I even told Jimmy that same thing at the beginning of the trial when he asked how he could prove his innocence. But somehow, I forgot." Luana winced. "I guess it was the excitement of defending my first client." She gave her mother a sheepish smile.

"Don't be embarrassed about that, honey," said Mrs. Porcello. "I've been there myself many times, especially at the beginning of my career."

"What if Jimmy did destroy Jenny's doll? What then, Mom? How do I defend him?"

"Our clients deserve a vigorous defense, innocent or guilty. One of your best strategies is to poke holes in the plaintiff's case. You try to show why any evidence they present is unreliable or why it could just as easily point to someone else's guilt. You want to point your jury—or, in this case, your judge—in another direction. Get them to view the evidence in a way that favors your client."

"I think I understand. Even if Jimmy is guilty, I make them fight to prove it. But what if he's innocent? He says he is, but a lot of evidence makes him look guilty." Luana sat up and wrapped her arms around her legs, resting her chin on her knees.

"Do you believe him?" her mother asked.

Luana hesitated, then gave a firm nod of her head. "Yes, I do. I had my doubts for a moment, but I know Jimmy. He would never lie. Not even to get out of trouble."

"Well, maybe you should review the evidence to see if it points to the identity of the real perpetrator."

"What?" Luana lifted her head.

"It's likely some of the evidence points to the identity of the actual guilty person. After all, one thing is certain; *someone* destroyed the doll."

Luana's eyes sparkled. "Mom, you're a genius! Look for clues pointing to who destroyed Rebecca. Why didn't I think of that?"

Renee Porcello laughed. "Genius? No, never that. But I have been doing this for a long time. Remember, it's only your first trial, so give yourself a break." She stood up, leaned over, and kissed Luana's cheek. "Don't stay up too late. You'll need to be fresh and alert to present

Jimmy's case tomorrow."

"Good night, Mom." She hugged her mother. "And thanks."

"Good night, baby."

❖ ❖ ❖

The following morning, Luana, Phoebe, and Jimmy sat at the defense table, waiting for the other children to arrive. The three friends had agreed to meet early to discuss strategy before Luana presented Jimmy's case to the court.

"So that's the plan," said Luana. "We'll poke holes in their evidence."

"Declan's eyewitness testimony is hard to disprove," said Phoebe.

"I think Luana did a fantastic job weakening his testimony yesterday." Jimmy took off his glasses and wiped the lenses with the hem of his blue t-shirt. "Sure, he saw me take an ax to a doll, but he couldn't say what type of doll it was. He certainly couldn't say it was Rebecca. And I'll testify it was Kid Kenny." He finished cleaning his glasses and returned them to his face.

"True," said Luana. "And Declan even admitted the toy Phoebe was holding—your Kid Kenny doll—resembled the one he saw you chopping on

Sunday. By the way, that glue of yours is amazing, Jimmy! Your Kid Kenny is almost as good as new."

He blushed. "Thanks. But it's not as good as I hoped it would be. It only works on paper and—"

"That all sounds good," Phoebe said. "But you've got to admit it's quite a coincidence that on the very day Jimmy hacks a doll into pieces, someone rips the head off his *sister's* doll!"

"You're right, but all we can do is try our best to show the weaknesses in the evidence," said Luana. "And don't forget, my mom said we should reexamine all the evidence for clues to the person who destroyed Rebecca."

"Hmm." Phoebe stared into the distance, mentally reviewing all the evidence presented in court. "I can't see how any of it points to a specific person," she said after a while.

"We'll just have to wait and see how things develop," said Luana. "In the meantime, Jimmy, was there anyone else—?"

She stopped speaking as Mary Beth, Jenny, and Ashley entered the courtroom.

"Hey, guys," the newcomers said as they approached the trio.

"Hey," Phoebe, Luana, and Jimmy said in reply. Within minutes, the other children arrived, and Heather called the court to order. "Miss Luana, are you ready to begin?"

"I am, Your Honor."

"Very good. You may proceed."

Luana moved to the lectern and placed a notepad on its surface. "I call Jimmy Corbett to the stand." Once Jimmy took the oath and sat down, Luana began her direct examination.

"Mr. Jimmy, you saw when your sister testified about the many times you'd broken her toys in the past. Do you admit to all the incidents she listed in court?"

"Yes, I do. Well, all except for Rebecca. I did not break Rebecca."

"Jenny testified that you were working on an invention in your shed the day someone destroyed Rebecca. Tell us about that morning."

"I was trying to create a new type of glue. I hoped to produce one that would bond any material: fabric, wood, plastic, acrylic—anything. Anyway, I got to where I was ready to test it, but I needed something to try it on. I couldn't find anything in the shed, so I checked the backyard, looking for something broken. I saw Jenny having a tea party with her doll, Rebecca, and asked her if she had any broken toys, but she said she didn't."

"What did you do then?"

"I returned to the shed. When I came out again, I didn't see Jenny. I went inside the house to look for something to test my glue. I couldn't find anything broken, so when I discovered my old Kid Kenny doll buried in the bottom of my toy box, I decided to use him instead. I fetched the ax from the garage, took Kid outside, and chopped him in two. That must have been when Declan saw me."

"Think back, Mr. Jimmy. Does anything about that day stand out to you?"

Jimmy carefully considered her question, then shook his head. "No, everything seemed normal. Mom was in the kitchen, baking brownies for a charity bake sale. Dad was out golfing with Colin." He chuckled. "Dad says he's determined that at least one of his children share his love for the game, and since neither Jenny nor I care for it, he's now focusing all his efforts on Colin. Anyway, it was a typical Sunday; everyone was doing their usual thing." He gave a lopsided grin. "Well, all except for Rufus. He was having a lazy Sunday. Usually, he's off somewhere getting into trouble, but that day he was lying around napping."

Luana glanced up from jotting a note on her

pad. "Rufus? You mean Mrs. Cuthbert's dog?"

"Yes," said Jimmy. "He spends a lot of time at our house. Poor Mrs. Cuthbert is too old to deal with him, so my parents volunteered to have Jenny and me help take care of him. He has a few bad habits but is a sweet dog."

Luana dug inside a canvas bag she had brought to court and removed a doll. "Your Honor, I ask that the court label this item as defense one for identification."

"The bailiff will label the item defense one," said Heather.

"Thank you, Your Honor. Mr. Jimmy, do you recognize defense one?"

"I do," he said. "It's my Kid Kenny doll."

"Is this the Kid Kenny doll you say you cut–?" Luana's eyes riveted to a note she'd doodled on her pad. *Review the evidence and see who else it could point to.* She dislodged a braid from her ponytail and wrapped it around her finger. *Who else?*

"Miss Luana, is there a problem?" Heather's voice broke into Luana's thoughts.

"Um, no, Your Honor. I'm sorry. I just had a thought. I'll continue."

"Please do," said Heather.

"I'm sorry, Mr. Jimmy. As I was saying, is this

the Kid Kenny doll you cut in half on Sunday?" said Luana.

"Yes, it is."

Who else? Who else? Luana's thoughts spun as she continued toying with the braid.

"Miss Luana?" Heather said.

"Hmm?"

"Are you going to continue?"

"Er, yes, sorry, Your–" *That's it!* "Your Honor, could I have a brief recess?" Luana's eyes shone.

"You're acting strangely." Heather studied Luana through narrowed eyes. "I guess a short recess would be all right. How much time do you need?"

"Maybe we could resume after lunch? Oh, and if we could meet at Phoebe's house, that would be great!"

The other children gawked at Luana.

"She's lost her mind," Mary Beth said in a stage whisper to Jenny. "The strain of trying to prove Jimmy innocent must have gotten to her."

"I believe you're about to lose your case, Mary Beth." Phoebe smirked. She knew Luana's distraction meant her friend was on to something.

While this exchange was taking place, Heather

declared the court in recess. They were to meet back at Phoebe's house after lunch.

"Let's go, Pheebs." Luana grabbed her backpack from under the defense table where she'd stored it earlier.

Jenny sprang to her feet and marched over to confront Luana, slamming her hands on her hips. "What's going on?"

"You'll see." Luana winked.

CHAPTER 8

Digging for the Truth

THE KIDS GATHERED in Phoebe's backyard, waiting to get started.

"This is ridiculous, Luana," Heather grumbled. She glanced down at her brand-new white sneakers, thinking maybe she should've changed her shoes. Of course, she hadn't known Luana intended to drag them into the woods. *If my shoes get dirty, I will quit this stupid court.* Heather scowled. "Court is in session." She looked around for somewhere to bang her gavel. A gleam entered her eyes when her gaze finally settled on Jake's head.

Noticing the expression on his sister's face, Jake leaped back several paces out of her reach.

Heather gave him a dirty look.

"What are we waiting for?" Jenny demanded.

"Get started, Luana," Heather snapped.

"OK, everyone," said Luana. "If you would all follow Phoebe."

Phoebe walked toward the conservation land adjoining her yard.

"Where are we going?" asked Mary Beth.

"Everything will become clear soon enough if I'm right," said Luana.

Several minutes later, Phoebe came to a halt. "Here we are." She motioned to a mound of dirt that appeared to have been disturbed recently. "This is it."

Ashley wrinkled her nose. "You brought us out here to show us a pile of dirt?"

"Just wait and see." Phoebe's eyes twinkled.

"You're up, Jimmy," said Luana.

Jimmy took the shovel he was carrying and started digging. After a few moments, he felt the shovel hit something. "I think I've found it!" He dug faster. After removing another couple of shovelfuls of dirt, he stopped and peered into the hole he'd dug. "Wow!"

The rest of the group moved closer to get a better look. They could see a bunch of items in the opening.

"Hey, that's my journal!" cried Mary Beth. "I've

been searching all over for that." She pointed to a small, leather-bound book, all tattered and covered with dirt, lying on top of the heap.

"You haven't been searching for it at all," said Ashley. "You accused *me* of taking it."

While the sisters argued, Luana crouched in the shallow opening and sifted through the collection. She briefly examined each item before tossing it aside. Finally, she found what she wanted. "Here it is!" She raised her hand, waving the object she held back and forth, her face beaming.

"Ew!" Mary Beth made a face. "What is that?"

Standing, Luana brushed off the dirt and moved aside clumps of matted hair covering the object.

Before she had completed the task, Jenny screeched, "It's Rebecca's head!" She screwed up her face. "I don't understand. What is it doing *here*?"

"Perhaps you'd like to explain, Miss Luana," said Heather.

"I'd be happy to, Your Honor." Luana rested the doll's head on a nearby rock and dusted the dirt from her hands.

"Ooh, this is like a Perry Mason moment!" Mary

Beth danced in place.

"Who's Perry Mason?" asked Jake. "Is he in our class?"

"No, Jake," said Ashley. "He's an amazing lawyer in an old television series." She waved a hand dismissively when she saw her friends' blank faces. "Oh, never mind. It's not important. Let's listen to what Luana has to say."

"Thanks, Ashley." Luana smiled. "From the beginning, I focused on the wrong thing in this case. I wanted to prove Jimmy's innocence. In doing so, I forgot one of the basic principles of law: the *plaintiff* must prove the defendant's guilt; the defendant does not need to prove his innocence. I got so caught up in trying to disprove Jenny's case that I forgot to ask the one question I should have asked from the beginning: if not Jimmy, then *who*? If Jimmy was innocent—and I believed he was—*someone else* must have destroyed Rebecca. We all know how much Jenny loves Rebecca, so she didn't do it. But the only other person who had access to the doll was Jimmy. *Or was he?*

"I'm ashamed to say I didn't even consider who else it could be until I talked to Mom. She told me to reexamine the evidence to find its weaknesses and see if it pointed to the identity of the real offender. That's when I reviewed the evidence and immediately realized there had been clues to the real culprit's identity from the start." She extended a hand to Jake. "May I please have Rebecca's body?"

Jake removed the doll from his backpack and handed it to her. At Luana's suggestion, he had brought the toy along on the court's impromptu field trip.

"Thanks." Undressing the doll, Luana pointed to the body. "Remember these dents all over the chest, stomach, and legs? Phoebe pointed them out the first time we examined the doll, but we couldn't figure out what had caused them. Then there's this hole in the tummy." She touched a finger to the puncture in the doll's stomach.

"Oh yeah," said Jake. "An ax couldn't have made those marks."

"Exactly, Jake," said Luana. "Those were the first clues that someone other than Jimmy committed the crime. Why would Jimmy put holes in the doll if all he wanted was to test his glue? He wouldn't. But Declan testified he saw Jimmy chop a doll in two. Of course, he couldn't say *which* doll Jimmy axed, but his testimony suggested that the doll he saw was Rebecca.

"However, if you believe Rebecca was the doll Declan saw Jimmy cut in two, how did she get these jagged edges on her neck?" Luana pointed to the marks around the doll's severed neck. "See?"

"An ax wouldn't have made rough edges, would it?" asked Lindsey in her quiet voice.

"No, it wouldn't, Lindsey," said Luana. "Remember, Declan said he saw Jimmy take 'one swing, and the two pieces flew in opposite directions.' A single blow of an ax did not cause these edges. They are too uneven. One blow from an ax would leave smoother cut lines. But then, Jimmy had another problem: his long history of destroying toys. True, he had never denied breaking a toy in the past—even when there wasn't an eyewitness—but that was *before* his parents decided he would have to pay to replace any toy he broke. And as Jenny pointed out in her testimony, none of those toys had been nearly as expensive as Rebecca."

"Yeah," said Jenny. "That's what I said." She stuck her nose in the air.

"It is a powerful reason to lie, Jenny, and for a moment—just a moment—I, too, doubted Jimmy. But I couldn't bring myself to believe he would lie.

It's just not in his character."

Jenny rolled her eyes and snorted.

"So this brings me back to the original question," said Luana. "If not Jimmy, then *who*? It came to me during Jimmy's testimony. He said he'd found his Kid Kenny doll buried in the bottom of his toy chest. *Buried*. That's when it hit me! There was someone else in the yard that day, someone who has a habit of taking people's stuff and running off with it—someone who has a habit of *burying* the things he steals!"

The children's eyes darted back and forth, their expressions puzzled. Only Phoebe and Jimmy knew to whom Luana was referring.

"I'm talking about Rufus," said Luana. "*He* is the one who has been snatching people's stuff in the neighborhood. Jimmy testified Rufus was in the backyard with him on Sunday afternoon. Jenny said she left Rebecca sitting at the tea-table while running an errand for her mother. Rebecca was within easy reach of Rufus. He likes to chew on things, which explains the dents on Rebecca's body and the hole in her stomach. Jenny testified Rebecca was wet and covered with a sticky substance. Dogs' saliva is sticky. Put it all together, and it makes sense."

"Wow!" Jake's eyes bugged out. "Rufus?"

Ashley shook her head. "I never would have thought of Rufus."

"I don't believe it." Mary Beth looked dumbfounded.

"I figured if Rufus had removed the head, he would have buried it somewhere," said Luana. "I remembered Phoebe telling me she'd chased after him and caught him digging a hole when he'd taken off with her sister's flute. Dogs typically have favorite holes they use over and over. So the chances were that if he had buried Rebecca's head, he buried it in the same spot where he'd tried to bury Penny's flute.

"So Phoebe, Jimmy, and I came out here to look for Rufus's hole. Phoebe had a fairly good idea of where it was after her previous run-in with him. Once we found it, I decided it would be best to bring you all here, so you could see for yourselves where Rebecca's head has been this entire time." Luana's face wreathed in smiles as she looked around at her friends, taking in their reaction to what she'd told them.

Just then, Rufus came barreling from among the trees, headed in their direction. In his mouth, he carried a baseball glove. As soon as he saw them, he stopped.

Jenny scowled and shouted, "Bad dog, Rufus!"

Rufus whined and dropped the glove on the ground. They could see the letters J.C. printed on it.

"Hey, that's my baseball glove!" Jake exclaimed.

Everyone burst out laughing.

"Well, that clinches it," said Heather. "You can't argue with the facts. So, if there are no objections, Miss Mary Beth, I intend to rule in favor of the defense."

Mary Beth glanced at Jenny, who shook her head and said, "I have no objection. Obviously, Rufus is the real culprit." She gave her brother a sheepish look. "I'm sorry I didn't believe you, Jimmy. I was so upset about losing Rebecca that I lost my head." She grimaced. "No pun intended. Can you ever forgive me?"

"Don't give it another thought," said Jimmy to

his twin.

"We have no objections, Your Honor," Mary Beth said.

"Very good. It is the opinion of this court that the defendant is innocent of the charge against him. And let this be a lesson to you, Miss Jenny. It's never good to jump to conclusions without having all the facts. OK, we're done here. Bailiff, you may return the items of evidence to their owners. The Kids Court is adjourned." Heather banged the gavel on a nearby tree trunk for emphasis. "Nice work, everyone."

So it wasn't Jimmy. Lindsey shook her head in disbelief. Throughout the trial, she'd worked hard typing everything on her computer. *All that work for nothing!*

"Don't worry, Jen." Jimmy put his arm around his sister's shoulder. "We'll replace Rebecca. I've got some savings. Maybe we can pool our money together and convince Mom and Dad to chip in."

"It's good of you to offer, Jimmy, especially after everything I've put you through. But Rebecca was one of a kind, you know? I can never replace her. I'll just have to be happy with my memories."

❖ ❖ ❖

After all the other children had departed a while later, Luana, Heather, and Phoebe stood in the Chens' front yard, discussing the trial's outcome.

"Who would have thought," said Heather, "that the dog did it?"

"Well, I, for one, am not surprised," Phoebe said. "I've always known Rufus is a menace to society!"

Luana chuckled. Two boys walking up the street toward them drew the girls' attention. The boys were dragging a demolished go-kart between them. It was Declan Mathias and Greg Foster. As the boys approached, the girls could hear them arguing.

"I didn't cause the accident, Greg. I'm telling you, there's something wrong with the go-kart!" said Declan.

"There's absolutely nothing wrong with my kart," Greg shot back. "You lost control when you jerked the steering wheel too hard."

"I did not!"

Heather sighed and put her arms around the girls' shoulders as the two boys continued arguing. "Looks like the Kids' Court will need to be in session again, ladies—soon!"

If you enjoyed this story, please leave a review giving it two thumbs up! Scan the QR code to go directly to the Amazon review page.

Continue reading for a sneak peek at Greg and Declan's story in *The Go-KartAstrophe.*

A KIDS' COURT WHODUNIT

WHODUNIT

THE GO-KARTASTROPHE

BY CARON PESCATORE

CHAPTER 1

Dollars and Sense

"HOW MANY TIMES do I have to tell you?" Declan Mathias shouted. "*It wasn't my fault!*"

"So what are you saying, Dec? The kart ran into the tree by itself?" Greg Foster scoffed.

"Something was wrong with the go-kart," said Declan. "I couldn't turn the wheel."

"Oh, please," said Greg. "I'd say the problem was you turned the wheel too hard. I saw you wrench it. That's what caused the kart to spin out of control. There was absolutely nothing wrong with it before that. But now it's in pieces, thanks to you."

Declan rolled his eyes. Greg was his best friend, but his tendency to exaggerate—which he often did—was beyond annoying. This was especially true when Greg told stories about his various athletic achievements. The go-kart was most definitely *not* "in pieces."

Next door, eleven-year-old Luana Porcello sighed. "Those two have been arguing nonstop ever since Declan crashed Greg's go-kart two days ago," she said to her best friend, Phoebe Chen. The two girls were lying out by the pool in Luana's backyard.

After they'd spent the morning helping Luana's mom clean the attic, the girls had planned to have a relaxing afternoon. Unfortunately, the ongoing argument next door shattered their peace.

"What's the big deal, anyway?" said Phoebe. "Why don't they just fix it? I mean, they're the ones who built the stupid thing in the first place." She rolled her light-brown eyes as she sat up and gathered her midnight-black hair into a ponytail, securing it on top of her head with a dark-blue scrunchy she slid from her right wrist.

Luana chuckled, the dimples in her cheeks popping. "I don't think it's that simple, Pheebs. It sounds like the go-kart needs major repairs, and Greg doesn't have the money to fix it."

They could hear the boys still going at it in the

background.

"You messed up and wrecked my kart," said Greg. "Now, you need to pay to fix it."

"I don't care what you say," said Declan. "The go-kart wasn't working right. It kept going straight, even though I spun the steering wheel. That's why it ran into the tree. I'll go fifty-fifty with you on the repairs, but that's it. And you're lucky I'm willing to do that much. You gave me a defective go-kart to drive. I could have been seriously hurt if I hadn't jumped out before it crashed."

"You've got some nerve!" Greg bellowed. "My go-kart is not 'defective.' You're so overly dramatic. First, you beg me to let you drive the kart, then you smash it to smithereens, and now you're whining like a baby about injuries you don't have." He ticked off Declan's offenses on his fingers as he listed each one.

"I did not beg you to drive the go-kart, and I'm not a baby! And who are *you* to call *me* overly dramatic?" Declan said. "You're the one who's blowing the damage to the kart out of proportion. It's not 'smashed to smithereens'—not even close. All it has is a bent frame and a broken steering column. You should be thanking me. If I hadn't slowed down before it hit that tree, the cart would really be in pieces." He shook his head. "You know what? Forget it. I didn't cause the accident, so I'm not giving you a dime. And that's that!" He crossed his arms and jutted his jaw.

"Fine! I'll have my dad call yours. Then we'll see who'll pay for the repairs. One thing's for certain. I'm not dipping into *my* savings to pay for it. Every penny I have is for the class ski trip this winter. There's no way I'm passing up on that!" The annual ski trip was the highlight of the eighth-grade school year, and both boys were eagerly looking forward to the three-day excursion.

"Oh, dear. It's getting ugly between those two." Luana's mouth turned down at the corners. She hated hearing the boys fight. They were best friends and had been inseparable since Declan moved into the neighborhood six years ago. "Perhaps we should see if we can help."

Phoebe gawked at her. "Help? How?"

Luana stared into space, twisting a long dark braid around her fingers—a habit she had whenever she was anxious, upset, or preoccupied. She bolted upright after a few moments; her entire face lit up.

"Oh, no." Phoebe groaned. "I know that look. It

usually means work—for me!"

Luana giggled. "Come on, Pheebs. I just thought we should offer to hear the boys' case in the Kids' Court. What do you think?"

Phoebe's eyes shone. "That's a great idea, Lu!" She sprang from her lounge chair and marched across the yard.

"Hey, where are you going?" Luana called after her.

"To talk to the boys," Phoebe yelled over her shoulder. "There's no time like the present—the sooner they go to court, the sooner we'll get our peace back!"

It was just like Phoebe to charge ahead without thinking. Her impetuous nature had gotten her into trouble more than a time or two.

But Luana had to admit her friend had a point. *The sooner we help the boys settle their argument, the sooner we can get back to relaxing,* she thought. Chuckling to herself, Luana headed next door, following at a slower pace. As she neared the Fosters' garage, she could hear Phoebe's voice.

"You two need to quit arguing! I can't hear myself think over all the bickering."

"We aren't bickering," Greg retorted. "We're having a serious discussion. But I wouldn't expect a little kid to understand the difference."

"Who are you calling a little kid? I'm not the one whining over a toy."

"My go-kart is not a toy!" said Greg, sounding outraged. "It's a motorized veh—"

"Yeah, yeah, yeah! Whatever. I don't care if it's a Lamborghini made of pure gold. I want you two to keep it down so I can get some peace."

"Um, Pheebs." Luana stood by the open garage door, peeking in. "We came over here to help . . . remember?"

"Help?" said Declan. "How can you help?"

"We overheard your—er—conversation," said Luana, advancing into the garage.

"Yeah. No doubt the entire neighborhood heard you." Phoebe's upper lip curled as she eyed the two boys.

"I thought perhaps you would consider taking your case to court." Luana bit the inside of her cheek and crossed the fingers of one hand behind her back.

"Court?" Greg knitted his brows. "I'd love to take Declan to court. Someone needs to make him pay for the damage to my go-kart. But what court would take my case?"

"A few of us started the Kids' Court," said

Luana. "It's a court *by* kids *for* kids."

To find out how Luana helps the boys save their friendship scan the QR code to get your copy of The Go-KartAstrophe today!

THE LOST LOCKET
A Phoebe Chen Mystery

Eight-year-old Phoebe Chen has her first case to crack. Can you help?

Phoebe loves figuring things out—deciphering puzzles, unscrambling word games, and anything that involves brainstorming. Her fondest wish is to solve mysteries like Nancy Drew—or her police detective father. So when a friend raises the alarm over a missing necklace, Phohjebe jumps at the chance to follow in her idol's footsteps and offers to take on the case.

Enlisting the aid of her BFF, Luana, Phoebe gets to work searching for clues, interviewing witnesses, and compiling a list of suspects. But when the evidence seems to implicate a friend, Phoebe realizes being a junior detective isn't all fun and games. Phoebe must find concrete evidence before she points the finger. Can she do it, or will the miscreant get away with their dastardly plot?

Do you want to know what happens in Phoebe's case? Then turn the page to find out how you can get your **free** copy of *The Lost Locket!*

Subscribe to Caron Pescatore's newsletter and get your free copy of *The Lost Locket*! Just scan the QR code.

AUTHOR'S NOTE

Thank you so much for reading *The Doll Dilemma*! I hope you had as much fun reading the story as I had writing it. Wasn't that a great idea Luana had, starting a neighborhood kids' court? You know, you could do it too!

If you enjoyed *The Doll Dilemma*, please consider leaving a review on Amazon or your favorite online bookstore and Goodreads, BookBub, and any other online book review website you may frequent. Reviews are a great way to help other readers discover new books!

Do you have a cool idea for a character's name or a case for the Kids' Court? Then send me an email at caronpescatore@gmail.com. I would love to hear it!

Sign up for my newsletter to ensure you don't miss any upcoming releases, book sales, or other news. Scan the QR code on the previous page to subscribe and get your copy of *The Lost Locket*.

I adore hearing from my readers, so please connect with me @caronpescatore on Facebook, Twitter, TikTok, or Instagram.

ABOUT THE AUTHOR

CARON PESCATORE was born in the United Kingdom. She spent her childhood in Jamaica before migrating to the United States. After practicing as a registered nurse for several years, she entered law school, getting her J.D. in 2001. She worked as an attorney for years before leaving the profession to become a stay-at-home mom—her most challenging career to date. Ms. Pescatore is passionate about justice and fairness for all, a sentiment that led, in part, to her decision to write the A Kids' Court Whodunit series. Her favorite pastimes are reading, writing, and watching true-crime shows. At present, Ms. Pescatore lives in Florida with her husband and children.

Glossary

Adjourn: To take a break

Attorney: A person licensed to practice law; give legal advice; and speak on behalf of people in court

Bailiff: An officer in a court who keeps the peace and order and protects the judge

Bench trial: A trial where the judge decides the outcome of the case instead of a jury

Court reporter: A type of secretary who works in a court and keeps a record of everything said by typing it down

Cross-examination: Questioning of a witness by the lawyer who did not call the witness to court

Damages: A sum of money awarded to a person to make up for a loss or injury

Defendant: A person accused of wrongdoing in a court of law

Direct examination: Questioning of a witness by the lawyer who called the witness to court

Evidence: Facts and information that help the court figure out the truth of what happened in a particular case

Gallery: The area in the courtroom where visitors

to the court can sit and observe the proceedings

Judge: A public official who decides cases in a court of law

Jury: A group of people (usually 6 or 12) who listen to the evidence in a trial and decide the outcome

Plaintiff: A person who brings a claim against another in a court of law

A Preponderance of evidence: The amount of proof the plaintiff must bring to court to convince the judge or jury that the defendant is guilty

Proffer: An offer of proof by a party to the court telling why evidence is essential to the case to convince the court to allow the evidence to be presented

Rest: A party rests when he finishes presenting evidence to the court

Testify: To give evidence as a witness in court

Testimony: a formal statement issued in a court

Trial: A court procedure where facts are presented to a judge or jury to decide the defendant's innocence or guilt

Witness: A person who gives evidence in court

Verdict: The outcome in a case deciding who wins and who loses

Made in United States
Troutdale, OR
11/07/2024

24515614R00071